The Mystery Kitten

The Mystery Kitten

by Holly Webb
Illustrated by Sophy Williams

tiger tales

For Hannah

tiger tales
5 River Road, Suite 128, Wilton, CT 06897
Published in the United States 2020
Originally published in Great Britain 2020
by the Little Tiger Group
Text copyright © 2020 Holly Webb
Illustrations copyright © 2020 Sophy Williams
Author photograph © Charlotte Knee Photography
ISBN-13: 978-1-68010-475-2
ISBN-10: 1-68010-475-6
Printed in the USA
STP/4800/0339/0620
10 9 8 7 6 5 4 3 2 1

For more insight and activities, visit us at www.tigertalesbooks.com

Contents

Chapter One
A New Beginning

This is a very strange way to start Christmas, Elsa thought. School had finished the day before, and she felt like they should be making cards or doing Christmassy cooking. Instead, she was dashing around trying to remember which box she'd put her purple sweater in, and where her tiny china cats were.

The whole house felt empty—just

boxes and boxes waiting to go in the moving truck later that morning. Her bed was still in the room she shared with her sister Sara, but she'd slept in a sleeping bag last night because all the sheets and blankets and pillows were packed.

It was exciting, but scary, too. The new house was a long way away—two hours' drive. Dad was starting a new job after Christmas, and Elsa and Sara would be going to new schools. *Everthing* was new.

"Elsa, how are you doing? Is everything packed?" Dad put his head around the bedroom door. *He looks so happy*, Elsa thought. Maybe a little stressed, too. The last few days had been really busy.

"I think so." Elsa turned around slowly, inspecting the odd, bare bedroom.

"Are you looking forward to having your own room at the new house?" Dad grinned. "No more complaining about Sara's clothes being everywhere."

Elsa nodded. She'd wanted her own room forever. But now that it was finally happening, she didn't know how it would feel to sleep on her own every night. When Sara went to sleepovers, it was always really weird without her.

"Come on downstairs, sweetheart," Dad told her. "You need to have some breakfast. It's going to be a long day." Elsa followed him, but as Dad headed down the stairs, she stopped for a moment in the doorway of her room, looking back. "It will be good," she told herself, crossing her fingers. "It will…."

The kitten stumbled over the dusty floorboards, meowing angrily. He was hungry, and he didn't know where everyone had gone. He'd fallen asleep half wrapped in an old sheet in the far corner of the attic. He liked it there— his four brothers and sisters squirmed and stomped and wriggled so much that sometimes it was good to sleep a little farther away. He was sick of them sitting on top of him.

Usually his mother came and shooed him back to the nest she'd made for them in a box of old clothes, but this morning, he'd woken up on his own. The attic was freezing, and the kitten shivered miserably as he wandered around looking for his family. He stumbled and sniffed and meowed, but there were no kittens hiding behind the boxes, or waiting to leap from under the battered old armchair.

Everyone was gone. The kitten stood gazing at their old nest—he could smell his mother and the other kittens. He could even see the dips and hollows where they'd snuggled down the night before. He scrambled unhappily over the torn edge of the box and squirmed into a ragged sweater, trying to warm himself up.

One of his brothers or sisters had dropped a piece of cooked chicken that their mother had carried upstairs for them, and he could smell it. He nosed it out eagerly and gobbled it up. Then he lay curled up in the sweater and waited for his mother to come back to him. He knew she would come back soon. He was sure.

Elsa sat cross-legged in the middle of her bed, looking around her new room. It was so big! When they'd come to view the house, the room had been full of furniture and a little cluttered. It had been hard to imagine what it would be like with her things in it. Dad had promised that she could help him paint the walls, but there was a lot of other stuff that needed doing first.

"I think your room might be bigger

than mine." Sara put her head around Elsa's door and squinted, obviously trying to measure it in her head.

"I'm not swapping," Elsa said swiftly. She loved her room already, and she wasn't letting Sara have it. She had plans for it. Purple paint instead of the faded old wallpaper, and maybe some fairy lights. She could have those now if Dad gave her an advance on her allowance.

"It's okay." Sara grinned. "I like mine. It's got a ton of shelves and an old fireplace. It's cool."

"Have you done any unpacking?" Elsa asked, looking at the pile of boxes in front of the window. She'd put some of her clothes away, but that was all.

"All of it," Sara said smugly, and

Elsa sighed. She should get on with unpacking her things, but every time she opened a box, she just started thinking about their old house and her friends....

"The yard is great," Sara said, threading her way between the boxes and going to look out Elsa's window. "We could definitely have a dog now that we have a real yard. I'm going to keep working on Dad."

"You can't see the yard—it's dark," Elsa muttered. Sara really wanted a dog, but Elsa wasn't sure. She had a feeling that if they got a dog, her sister would always be dragging her out on long walks before school. But she did like the idea of snuggling up on the couch with an adorable, furry puppy.

"I can see parts of it," Sara insisted. "And there's a trampoline next door— did you see? So they must have kids, too."

Elsa nodded hopefully. Maybe they would go to the school she was starting at. She was in fourth grade, but Sara was eleven and in middle school, so Elsa wouldn't have her sister with her. She couldn't stop thinking about what it would be like, walking in on her own.

She shook herself and got up to open a box. It was harder to worry about things when she was busy.

"Will you help me put this stuff away?" she asked Sara pleadingly, but her big sister rolled her eyes.

"Not a chance. Sorry." She smirked at Elsa and whisked out of the room. Elsa sighed and unfolded the top of a box. It was actually fun, figuring out where to put everything. She just had to think of it as a new start, that's all.

They had pizza for dinner, but Dad had almost finished arranging the kitchen, and he said they'd start cooking regular meals again soon. "When we find the cookie cutters, you could make some of those gingerbread stars to hang up," he suggested. "And we need to get a Christmas tree." He smiled at Elsa. "That'll be fun, won't it? We could have it in front of the living-room window."

Elsa nodded and tried to smile back. She'd been really upset when Dad had first told them they needed to move for his work. She hadn't wanted to leave her friends—it just didn't seem fair. She was mostly used to the idea now, but Dad was still worrying about her.

"You're falling asleep," Dad said a few minutes later, taking a drooping slice of pizza out of Elsa's hand. "You go on up. I'll come and say good night in a minute."

Elsa yawned and nodded, but once she was out in the hallway, the pleasant sleepy feeling seemed to fade away. This house was so much older than their last one. It had odd creaky boards and patches of shadowy blackness that the lights didn't reach. As she put her foot on the first step, she heard a weird little noise, like scratching claws....

She scurried up the stairs in a sudden panic,

feeling as though something might be behind her. Was something watching her? Then she hurled herself through her bedroom door and scrambled into bed, panting and hugging her knees. If she was curled up small, whatever was following her up the stairs might not see....

After a minute or two, Elsa shook herself. Of course there hadn't been anything behind her. But there was something about this house. Something strange—as though she and Sara and Dad weren't the only ones here.

Elsa flinched a little as she heard voices downstairs, and then there was a rush of footsteps and Sara called, "Night, Elsa!" as she came past. Elsa caught her breath, and then giggled and went into the bathroom to brush her teeth. She was tired, that was all. She'd been half asleep and not thinking straight. Everything was fine. It would all be fine.

By the time her dad came up to check on her, Elsa was fast asleep.

She woke up much later, clutching at her comforter in panic. The room was so dark—much darker than the room she and Sara had shared before, where there was a streetlight right outside. This room was velvet-black, and she couldn't see a thing.

What had woken her? Elsa peered around, her breath coming fast, as if she'd been running. It was like that weird moment on the stairs all over again.

"Dad's right across the hall...," Elsa whispered to herself. She could wake him up in seconds. She just had to get out of bed....

Above her head, something scratched and pattered—and then cried out.

Elsa burrowed down under her comforter, pulling it over her head to make a safe little tent. She wasn't going *anywhere*....

Chapter Two
The Surprise

"There's no such thing as ghosts," Sara said, rolling her eyes.

"How do you know?" Elsa glared at her. Sara always thought she knew everything. Elsa wasn't sure she believed in ghosts, either, but there was definitely *something* going on.

"Because it's nonsense! You were just having a nightmare, that's all."

"Dreams can feel very real when you're in them," Dad agreed. "But the house doesn't seem spooky now in daylight, does it?" He was looking worried. He and Elsa and Sara had talked a lot about people dying, as the girls' mom had died when Elsa was two. Dad definitely didn't believe in ghosts. He'd told them so.

"What about when I was going up the stairs?" Elsa pointed out. "I wasn't asleep then. How could that weird noise have been a nightmare?"

Sara yawned and stretched. "It was probably the floorboards squeaking. Or the water pipes."

"That's very likely." Dad nodded. "The house *is* a little old and creaky."

Elsa jabbed her fork at her scrambled eggs. Sara sounded right—she always did—but Elsa still wasn't sure. There had been *something*, she knew it. Something watching ... waiting. Creaky boards were one thing, but somebody had to walk on them to make them creak, didn't they?

Sara glanced up suddenly, her face worried. "You don't think it was a

25

rat, do you?"

"It could have been," Dad said. Elsa wrinkled her nose. Natalie, her friend from school—her old school, she reminded herself—had two pet rats. They did claw and scratch around. She loved Natalie's rats—they were cuddly and funny—but she wasn't sure about the not-a-pet kind living in her house.

"Dad! Rats!" Sara was looking horrified now. She really didn't like rats or mice. Elsa had tried suggesting that rats would be good pets after she'd met Natalie's, but Sara had flat-out refused to ever, ever, ever have them in their bedroom. Dad hadn't been open to the idea, either, but he'd said he'd think about guinea pigs once they were settled.

"I'm sure if there were rats, the previous owner would have told us," Dad said. "Don't panic, you two. It was probably just a creaky board or the water pipes, like Sara said."

The kitten woke up from his nap and poked his nose out from under the old sweater, looking hopeful. Was his mother back? Was there more food? His whiskers shivered and twitched as he waited for his brothers and sisters to leap on top of him and lick him and nibble his ears. He wouldn't mind, not this time. His ears pricked up as he listened, ready to jump out and run to his mother....

But there was no one else in the attic.

The kitten's ears flattened slowly and he sniffed, trying to follow the fading scent of his mother and the rest of the litter. He scratched frantically at the old clothes, nuzzling under the layers as if he might find them at the bottom of the box. But there were only sweaters and scarves, and the box was cold.

Whatever the noise was that had woken him, it had come from downstairs.

The kitten wriggled out of the clothes again and stumbled over the side of

28

the box onto the floor, padding over to the doorway.

Whenever he'd tried to go through the door before, his mother had always shooed him back. Sometimes she'd even picked him up in her mouth, dragging him to the safety of the box nest. But his mother had been gone for so long this time, he was starting to think she wasn't coming back.

The kitten stood there, listening and sniffing the air. He could hear footsteps and voices coming from somewhere. Would there be food, too? He was so hungry now that his stomach hurt. He was sure he could smell food. He edged forward a little and looked out on to the tiny landing at the top of the attic stairs. The smell was even stronger out here.

There was definitely food down there.

Determinedly, the kitten padded across the landing to the top step and eyed the mountain of stairs below.

Elsa went back upstairs after breakfast to finish her unpacking—it was better than helping Dad get all the kitchen plates and mugs out of their bubble wrap.

She stood by the window for a few minutes, looking into the yard and wondering if she might see the kids from next door. But it was a little cold to be out on the trampoline, she supposed.

She'd started arranging the bulletin board from her old room yesterday, pinning on photos of her old friends.

The Surprise

The board was on the floor with photos scattered all over it, as well as cards and notes from Natalie and Lara and the others. She sat down in front of the board and picked up the little box of pushpins—Natalie had given her some cute ones as part of a good-bye present, with stars and flowers and hearts on the tops of them.

Elsa sniffed. She missed everyone so much already. Even if the trampoline did mean there were kids living next door, it wasn't ever going to be the same as her and Natalie and Lara. They'd been friends since preschool.

Then she frowned down at the board—it looked different. The photo of her and Natalie and Lara that she'd had in the middle was pushed off to the side, and the card from her teacher was on the floor under her desk.

For a minute Elsa thought it must have been Sara, but her sister wouldn't do that. Sara knew how upset she'd been about changing schools—Sara was sad about leaving her own friends, too. She and her sister argued a lot, but they were never mean to each other.

Elsa shivered. Dad and Sara had almost convinced her at breakfast. Rattling water pipes and squeaky boards, that's all it was. No ghosts. Now she wasn't so sure. *Something* had come in and messed up her board. Elsa looked over her shoulder at the door. She could hear Sara playing music in her room, and Dad was downstairs—everything seemed so normal. There couldn't be a ghost moving things around in her bedroom.

Could there?

Something scuffled under her bed and Elsa yelped, scrambling back toward the door. She was expecting some kind of monster to come leaping out at her, or a grayish misty presence, or maybe a spookily pale girl in a nightgown....

Instead, there was a squeak. A tiny, frightened sort of squeak.

Whatever the ghost wanted, it sounded even more frightened than she was, Elsa decided. Very, very slowly, she crouched down and peered at the space under her bed. She was tense, ready to spring up and run if there was some horrible creature under there—or even a cornered, angry rat.

Staring back at her were two glowing, bright green eyes. In the shadows under Elsa's bed, it almost looked as though they were floating. For a tiny fraction of a second, Elsa remembered a scary story that Lara had told on their class sleepover about a yellow-eyed goblin that climbed on your back in the middle of the night and stole your breath away—

and then she blinked, and her eyes got used to the shadows and she saw what it was.

There was a kitten under her bed. A tiny, furry, frightened black kitten.

Chapter Three
A New Friend

"Where did you come from?" Elsa breathed. "Oh, don't be scared…," she added as the kitten flinched back into the shadows. "It's okay. I'm friendly. I wonder who you belong to." Then she frowned. "Maybe you don't belong to anyone. Was it you making all those strange noises?" It would make sense— the scratching could definitely have been kitten claws, and the squeaky little cry, too. "Oh, kitten, we thought you were a rat...."

The kitten peered out at her anxiously, its eyes all black in the darkness now, with just a hair-thin rim of gold. It was very small and skinny, Elsa realized. So small that she wasn't sure it should be out on its own.

"Where's your mom?" she whispered. Then she nibbled her bottom lip. The kitten must have belonged to the previous owner of the house, the elderly lady she'd met weeks ago. She'd explained that she was moving because she couldn't manage the stairs anymore. She'd seemed so nice. Elsa couldn't imagine her abandoning a kitten, but how else could the poor little thing have been in the attic?

"You must be starving," Elsa whispered, wriggling backward and getting up slowly so as not to scare the kitten. "Just stay there a minute, okay? I'm going to get you something to eat." She slipped out and tiptoed downstairs, wondering if Dad was still in the kitchen. He'd said something about trying to fix the dripping tap on the sink. She wasn't sure she could argue for a snack, not just after breakfast, and she really didn't want to tell Dad there was a kitten in her bedroom. Not yet, anyway.

Luckily, her dad was unpacking books in the living room and didn't hear her creep past. It looked like he'd gotten distracted and started reading, which was good news. He wouldn't be coming to check on her for a while.

Elsa opened the fridge as quietly as she could, holding her breath as the door creaked, but there was still no sound from the living room. She grabbed a slice of ham, although that didn't seem like enough for a hungry kitten. A cat wasn't going to want grapes, or yogurt…. Then she remembered Grandma telling them that her cat Patches' favorite food was cheese. Elsa broke off a chunk and grabbed one of the plates that Dad had been unpacking, then she padded silently back past the living room. The stairs gave a huge groaning creak when she was halfway up and Elsa froze, but nothing happened—Dad must be deep in his book.

At last she slipped back into her room and crouched down to look for the kitten again. It was still huddled against the wall under her bed, and when it saw Elsa, it shifted worriedly and pressed itself even farther back.

"Are you hungry?" Elsa whispered. "Look what I've got. Do you like cheese? Or ham?" She showed the plate to the kitten and then tore off a piece of ham and held it out. Was she imagining it, or did the kitten's huge black ears flicker with interest?

"You probably don't want to come out just yet," Elsa said thoughtfully. She lay down on her front, and then slowly, slowly crept her hand under the bed. The kitten gave a breathy little squeak of fear.

"It's okay. Just leaving this for you." She dropped the piece of ham about halfway under the bed—not too close to the kitten. The poor thing was scared enough already. Then she squirmed back and watched hopefully. Was the kitten brave enough to come and get the food?

The kitten eyed the ham suspiciously for a moment, but he could smell it, and it smelled so good. He measured the distance between him and the food and the girl. She was very close…. But even as he was thinking it, he found himself creeping forward. He was just too hungry to wait. He gobbled down the scrap of ham with one eye firmly on the girl—if she moved, he could dart back.

But she didn't; she was absolutely still and quiet. And she had more food. He could see it on the plate right in front of her. More meat and something else....

The girl moved her hand and the kitten scuttled back, but she wasn't reaching out to grab him. All she did was tear off another piece of ham and drop it gently, just at the edge of the safe space under the bed. Closer to her this time.

The kitten took a little longer to decide what to do, but the smell of food was so enticing that he forgot he was scared. He padded forward, step by slow step, and gulped down the second piece. Then he sat, almost out in the open, peering forward at the plate. There was a lot more ham left—more than he'd had already. And whatever the other stuff was smelled just as good—rich and salty and delicious.

The girl whispered something, her voice gentle, and she reached for the food, crumbling the good-smelling stuff and scattering it on the floor right in front of him. He'd only have to set one paw out beyond the shelter of the bed. Just one paw.

He edged out, pressed low to the ground, his shoulders hunched up into nervous points. His pink tongue darted out, sweeping up the scraps of cheese, and his eyes widened delightedly at the taste. Was there more of it? He stared hopefully at the girl and then laid his ears back a little as she held out her hand to him, the delicious stuff right there in her palm.

So now he had to go close….

He put out another paw and shook himself as he came into the light of the room. The girl was just there, with the food so temptingly on her hand. If she moved suddenly, he could dash back to the bed, couldn't he? He crept all the way over to her and began to lick up the crumbs of cheese.

Elsa swallowed her giggles—the kitten was tickling her, its tongue working carefully over her fingers, making sure to find every tiny crumb. "Is the cheese good?" she asked, wishing she could pet it. The fur was a soft, fluffy kind of black, not smooth and shiny like some black cats she'd seen before. But maybe that was only because it was so little. Its tongue was bright, bright pink against the black of its fur.

"What about the rest of the ham?" she whispered gently. "Should I tear it up?" She reached out her other hand and picked up the half slice that was left, but the kitten didn't wait for her to make nice bite-sized pieces. It scrambled up onto her knee and grabbed for the food, trying to gulp down the whole piece at once.

Elsa sat like a statue. She hoped the kitten wasn't going to make itself sick, gobbling like that. It must be so hungry. When it had finished, the pink tongue worked thoroughly around its muzzle and whiskers to make sure it hadn't missed anything. Then it stopped and eyed her cautiously, as though it had just figured out that it was sitting on top of her. Elsa decided it was thinking about making a mad dash back to the bed. It padded its paws up and down thoughtfully on her knee, but it didn't move. Instead, it lifted up one front paw and began a careful wash, swiping its paw around its muzzle and ears, still with one eye firmly fixed on Elsa.

Very slowly, Elsa let out the breath she'd been holding. What was she going to do now?

She was just wondering if she dared to try petting the kitten when the doorbell rang, loud and shrill, and the kitten leaped off her lap and shot back under the bed again. Elsa sighed.

There was a faint yell from downstairs. "Girls? Can one of you get that? I'm under the sink—it's leaking!"

Elsa listened hopefully for Sara, but her sister still had her music playing, so she dashed downstairs and wrestled with the unfamiliar lock on the front door. When she finally got it open, there was a girl about her own age standing on the step, looking nervous. She smiled when she saw Elsa.

"Um … hi. I'm Lilly. From next door. I saw you looking out your window earlier and thought I'd come and say hi." She twisted her fingers together and gazed at Elsa shyly.

"Oh! I'm Elsa. We just moved in yesterday. Um, do you want to—" Elsa stopped suddenly. She'd been about to say "Do you want to come in?" but then she remembered the kitten in her bedroom. The secret, mysterious kitten that nobody knew about. Elsa's eyes widened in sudden horror.

The kitten that was in her bedroom with the door open! She turned to peer up the stairs, hoping that she'd closed it after all.

She hadn't.

She turned back to Lilly, biting her bottom lip. She had to get her to leave, before the kitten decided to make a run for it. What if it disappeared somewhere and she never saw it again? Or it wandered into Sara's room?

"Um, I'm really sorry, but I have to go," she muttered quickly, starting to shut the door.

"Oh … okay…." The other girl looked really hurt, Elsa realized as she closed the door. She supposed she had been a little rude. Well, very rude, actually. But she couldn't help it. "It was the girl next door coming to say hello!" she yelled to Dad, and then she raced back upstairs and flung herself down next to the bed. The little black kitten was nowhere to be seen.

Chapter Four
An Important Decision

Had the kitten gotten out of her room? Elsa sat up, looking around anxiously. Maybe it had dashed through the open door, back upstairs to the attic. She wasn't supposed to go up there—Dad said the floor wasn't safe—but she could go and put her head around the door….

A tiny rustling made her turn and

look at the pile of boxes, and she let out a soft sigh of relief. There were two black twitching ears poking out of the nearest box.

"What are you doing in there?" Elsa asked, going to peer in at the kitten. Now that she looked, she could see delicate scratch marks on the cardboard where it had scrambled its way up. "Are you still hungry? Are you looking for more food?"

The kitten stared back at her, and Elsa was sure it looked hopeful. "I can go and get some more," she suggested. "Oh, except Dad is in the kitchen now. We might have to wait a while." She eyed the kitten's tufted ears and green eyes and added, "I wonder if you're a girl kitten or a boy kitten.... I don't like calling you 'it.' Um … I'm going to guess you're a boy. But if I called you Pepper, that could be for a boy or a girl, couldn't it?"

The kitten clambered up onto Elsa's folded sweaters and made a friendly squeaking noise. He was definitely a lot less shy since she'd fed him, Elsa decided.

"I probably shouldn't have named you," she told him with a sigh. "I don't think you're going to be able to stay here, Pepper kitten. Dad doesn't want a cat, and neither does Sara. She's been begging to get a puppy forever, but I don't think that's going to happen. I might have persuaded Dad to get guinea pigs, but he's still only thinking about it."

The kitten wobbled across the sweaters so that he was a little closer to Elsa and then leaned over, bumping his head against her hand.

Elsa's eyes widened. Had she just imagined that? She hadn't dared to pet him—he seemed way too nervous and jumpy. But he had touched her! All on his own! "Thank you," she whispered, wondering if he'd do it again. He was looking up at her, his eyes shining brightly in the winter sun that was pouring through her window.

"I don't care if Dad and Sara don't want a cat," Elsa muttered. That tiny, quick touch of his velvet-soft fur had made all the difference. She still didn't think the kitten was her cat, but she definitely felt as if she was *his* person. "I'll just have to persuade them somehow." She wrinkled her nose. "Only—maybe not yet…. Dad is still a little stressed about the move, and I bet he's not happy about that leaking sink, either. It's not really a good time to tell him we've got a cat." She held her hand out a little closer

to the kitten, watching him hopefully.
Would he do it again?

There was a moment's pause, and
then the kitten rubbed the side of his
chin against her hand, his eyes closed.
And—yes! There was a tiny, breathy,
rumbling sound. Elsa could feel it, too,
shaking the kitten all over.

He was purring.

Elsa decided that she needed to
keep Pepper hidden for a few days,
at least. During lunch, she told Sara
and Dad that she was working on a
Christmas surprise and could they
please stay out of her room? Dad had
looked really happy, as if that meant

she must be settling in.

Actually, Pepper would be a great Christmas surprise, Elsa thought to herself in bed that night. She could put some ribbon on a cat collar…. She shifted her feet very slightly, just to feel the weight of a kitten on her toes again. She hadn't expected Pepper to sleep on her bed—she had taken the box of sweaters off the top of the stack and put it down on the floor to make it easier for him to climb into.

She'd done her best to make her bedroom into a proper kitten home. She'd spread some newspapers on the floor in the corner of her bedroom, hoping he'd know to use those instead of a litter box, and she'd told

Dad she was starving and needed an extra ham and cheese sandwich at lunchtime. She'd borrowed one of the plastic picnic plates and a little bowl for Pepper's water. It was going to be tricky sneaking food upstairs, but Dad was still busy sorting everything out. Sara was more likely to see what she was doing than he was.

Elsa had spent the afternoon trying to get to know the kitten better. She spent a long time feeding him the sandwich piece by piece, although he turned his nose up at the crusts. Then she rolled a ball of paper around for him to chase, and waved the piece of curly ribbon that Natalie had used to wrap up her good-bye present. It bounced up and down in a long, shiny coil, and the kitten

darted after it with huge leaps—Elsa figured that some of the time, he jumped his own height, or even higher.

"Did you have kitten brothers and sisters?" she'd asked him, laughing as he stomped away from her with the ribbon in his sharp little teeth. He probably missed having them to play with. He must miss them all the time, she realized sadly. And his mother, too.

When she'd gone to bed, she'd lifted

Pepper into the box of sweaters, but he'd clambered right out again and stood by her bed. When Elsa got in, he scrambled up after her, digging his claws into the comforter, and padded around curiously for a while before curling up by her feet.

Elsa sat up in bed, trying to see the kitten. His black fur settled into the shadows so completely that she could only see a faint round shape, but she could feel him. "How did you end up in the attic on your own?" she wondered again, but the only answer was faint kitten breathing.

Elsa lay back down, thinking about the day. The only thing that spoiled it was the hurt look on Lilly's face when she'd said she had to go.

Maybe Elsa should have explained. But she couldn't, really—could she? She'd only just met Lilly. She couldn't tell her an enormous secret, not when she didn't know her.

Still, Lilly had looked so upset. And it had been really nice of her to come over and say hello. Elsa sighed. Maybe she should go to Lilly's house and explain after all. It would be weird, but if she didn't do something, she'd have to live next door to somebody who thought she was mean for years and years. Lilly probably went to her new school, too. What if she told everybody that her new next-door neighbor was mean and unfriendly? Elsa's stomach twisted with horror.

"I'll have to do something," she muttered sleepily into her pillow. "Tomorrow. I'll think about it tomorrow. 'Night, Pepper."

The kitten snuffled and opened one eye. The girl kept on wriggling around, but she was very warm—and not as wriggly as a box full of kittens. It was good to be full of food, even though he missed his mother's milk and the comforting feeling of sucking and snuggling up against her. He still wondered where she was and where his brothers and sisters were, but the strange lost feeling wasn't quite as bad as it had been before.

He stretched out to his full length, padding his paws against the comforter, and then stomped along the bed, wobbling over the lumps and bumps of the bedding. The girl was fast asleep, breathing softly, her long hair spread over the pillow. He tapped at it with one paw, and she mumbled something in her sleep but didn't wake.

The kitten peered thoughtfully over the top of the comforter, drawn up close over her shoulders. Under there it would be very cozy. He nudged the comforter up a little with his nose and crept inside the soft darkness, snuggling up against the girl.

Warm. Full. Sleepy.

It was good.

Chapter Five
The Apology

The next morning, Elsa woke up incredibly cozy. They were still figuring out how to use the radiators in the new house, and it seemed to be icy or boiling, and nothing in between—her bedroom had been freezing on their first night. *Obviously Dad figured out how to make the radiators work*, she thought blissfully, still half asleep.

Then something wriggled next to her chin, and there was a small, purring snore.

Pepper was under the comforter with her, lying on his back with his paws on his tummy and his eyes closed tightly. Elsa had to put her hand over her mouth to keep herself from laughing and waking him up. "You're the best hot-water bottle," she whispered, gently tickling him under his furry chin. "I'm so lucky. Yesterday morning when I woke up, I didn't have a clue that soon there would be a kitten in my bedroom."

Then she sighed. She just remembered Lilly next door. She was going to have to do something—maybe go over and say she was sorry? But that would mean telling Lilly about the kitten, and she still wasn't sure she wanted to do that…. What if Lilly told her parents, and they told Dad? Elsa wriggled until she was half sitting up, and Pepper gave a whistling sigh, half opened one eye, and glared at her.

"I'm sorry," Elsa whispered. "It's okay. Go back to sleep." Under the comforter, the kitten scrambled up onto her tummy and curled himself into a tiny black knot with his back to her.

"That's telling me off," Elsa giggled. "I'm sorry, kitten. But I still don't know how I'm going to fix things with Lilly. Maybe I could get her to promise not to tell first. But I'm not sure I want to go over there. It would be too weird…."

Elsa sighed and stared vaguely around her room, thinking about getting dressed. It was a little too early to go visiting anyway. Then she blinked, peering over at her bulletin board, still only half done, with letters and photos scattered around it. "I could write Lilly a letter," she said, brightening up a bit. "I could write and explain that I didn't mean to be unfriendly—it was just that I was in the middle of unpacking...." The kitten turned to look at her over his shoulder, yawned hugely, and went back to sleep again.

Elsa rubbed his ears. "Yes, I know it's not a great excuse. But it's the best I've got...."

It was all very well deciding to write to Lilly, Elsa discovered, but it didn't make the letter easy to write. How was she supposed to explain to someone she'd only spoken to for a minute that she was sorry if she'd sounded rude, but she had a really important secret and she wasn't sure who she could trust? In the end, she wrote:

Dear Lilly,
This is Elsa from next door. I'm sorry I was a little weird and unfriendly yesterday. I'd really like to talk to you again. I had to go because I was worried about getting all my unpacking done. I'd like to be friends if you would.
From, Elsa

Elsa read the note and sighed. Either Lilly would read her letter and she'd come over so Elsa could talk to her—or she'd never want to talk to that odd girl next door ever again. She helpfully took a pile of packing paper that Dad had finished with out to the recycling bin, and dashed next door to stick her envelope through the mail slot in the front door. She heard it bump onto the floor and crossed her fingers hopefully.

"How's your Christmas surprise going?" Dad asked as she came back in. Elsa stared at him blankly for a moment before she remembered her excuse for spending so much time in her room.

"Um … it's okay," she muttered. "I'm not sure if you and Sara will like it, though…."

"I'm sure we will." Dad put his arm around her and kissed the top of her head. "I'm so glad you're feeling a little happier, Elsa. I really am."

Elsa hurried back upstairs to her room, feeling guilty. It was great that the mystery in the new house had turned out to be a kitten, but she wished she didn't have to lie to Dad about it. And when was she going to tell him the truth? She had meant it when she'd told herself she'd show Pepper to Dad "when he wasn't so busy with the move," but it was hard to see when that was actually going to be.

Pepper came running toward her looking hopeful, and Elsa laughed. He danced around her feet, padding at her legs with his front paws and putting on a show of being the hungriest kitten who ever lived.

"You probably are hungry," Elsa sighed, frowning at him. "I guess your mom was feeding you whenever you wanted. Growing kittens need a lot of food—and you're definitely growing. I'm sure you're bigger than you were yesterday. Plumper around the middle, anyway. It's okay—Dad made us BLT sandwiches as a treat." She pulled out the half sandwich she'd wrapped in a tissue and hidden in her pocket. "Dad put ketchup on it before I could stop him, so I hope you like it." But the kitten didn't look worried. His huge, bright green eyes were fixed on the sandwich as if he'd never seen anything so exciting.

Elsa fed the bacon to him slowly, in pieces, worried that otherwise, he'd wolf down the whole thing and be sick. But just as she was about to hand him the last piece, the kitten turned away from her, his ears twitching.

"What is it?" Elsa whispered. "Can you hear something? It's probably just Sara in the next room."

The kitten was looking toward Elsa's window, though, as if he thought there was something happening outside. And now that she thought about it, Elsa could hear something—a tapping sound. Maybe a bird hopping around on the roof? She looked out curiously but couldn't see anything. Then the tapping sound started again, sharp and distinct. It was coming from the house next door, she realized—from the window. Someone was tapping on the glass.

Elsa opened the window, struggling a little with the stiff handle, and leaned out to look. The two houses weren't built exactly the same, so where her window faced out to the yard, and had a little slope of roof underneath it, the next house stuck out farther, and there was a window in the side wall instead.

There was a piece of paper pressed up against it, and she could see Lilly behind it, peering at her.

I got your note. You were really mean yesterday! the piece of paper said.

Elsa flinched. So much for trying to make friends. Then she tore out a piece of paper from the pad on her desk and scribbled *I'm really sorry* in big letters. She held it out of her window to show Lilly, and then ducked back inside and wrote *Didn't mean to be* on the back.

She looked across at Lilly, still framed in her own window. The other girl didn't look very impressed. She was chewing her bottom lip and frowning back at Elsa as though she didn't really know what to say.

Elsa was so busy watching Lilly and worrying that she almost missed the scratching, scraping noises by her elbow. There was a whisper of soft fur against her hand, and a curious black kitten put his front paws on the window frame and leaned out, wobbling as he sniffed the winter cold.

Elsa yelped, and Pepper glanced around at her in surprise, his paws suddenly sliding against the slippery frame. His ears flattened back and he hissed in panic, clawing wildly at the painted wood.

"Pepper!" Elsa yelped as she grabbed at him. It was like trying to catch a handful of water, or sand. He wriggled and twisted, and Elsa scraped her wrists against the roof tiles trying to grab hold. But at last she stepped back from the window, panting. Pepper was snuggled against her cardigan, and she could feel his heart hammering against his skinny little ribs. "It's okay," she whispered shakily. "It's all right. Oh, wow. I thought you were going to slide all the way down." There was a frantic tapping from the opposite window, and Elsa's eyes widened. So much for her secret.

The sign in the window now read *Are you okay?* But Lilly was wrenching at the window lock, and as Elsa watched, she pushed it open at last.

"Did you hurt yourself?"

"Um. I'm a little scratched. Not Pepper—the tiles."

"Is that his name? Pepper?"

"Yeah—but please don't tell your mom and dad. He's not mine. I mean, not really. He's a secret, like a mystery…. Oh, and don't shout too loudly, either—my sister's room is next to this one."

Lilly frowned again. She hesitated, and then she said, "Okay…. Can I come over?"

Pepper lay slumped in Elsa's lap, exhausted. He'd been chasing pieces of ribbon and a bouncy feather all morning with Elsa and the other girl, and then Elsa had built him an obstacle course out of boxes after lunch. Now he needed a nap. Elsa was tired, too, he thought. But happy. He could feel it in the way she was petting him, slow and soft, all relaxed.

He yawned, a yawn so huge that it stretched the muscles around his jaw, and then padded his paws up and down on Elsa's jeans to get them comfy. He sagged down, slumping onto Elsa's leg. She was so soft, and he was so sleepy.

Then his eyes popped open and his ears flattened back, and Elsa squeaked as the door banged open.

Pepper shot off her lap in fright,

darting under the bed to hide in the safe shadows. There was a second of silence and then a yell from the doorway. He cowered back even farther.

"What was that? Was it a rat?"

"No, Sara! Don't be silly!"

"You have a rat in your bedroom! I knew there was something. I thought I heard scratching noises!"

"It isn't a rat!"

Pepper pressed himself against the wall as he heard footsteps. He didn't like this noisy, screechy person. The girl who'd played with him earlier had been quiet and gentle, like Elsa. And they'd both given him cheese, which was definitely his favorite food. He watched anxiously as the strip of light at the edge of the bed darkened and two faces leaned down to peer in—Elsa and the loud person.

"Elsa … where did you get a kitten?"

Chapter Six
The Secret Is Out

Elsa wriggled back from the bed and sighed. "We'd better leave him for a little while. You scared him, screaming like that!" She looked accusingly at her big sister, and Sara rolled her eyes.

"You can't blame me, Elsa! I only saw it for a second, and it really did look like a rat darting under your bed. You know I hate them."

"Since when are rats black with furry tails?" Elsa demanded. "He doesn't look anything like a rat. And don't call him it. He's a boy kitten. Or I think he is."

"But Elsa, where did you get him?" Sara frowned. "Is he the secret Christmas surprise? Because Dad is not going to want a kitten for Christmas, I'm telling you now!"

"I didn't get him on purpose," Elsa said slowly, trying to think how she could explain. "You know those weird noises I said I heard? All the scratching around in the attic?"

"That was a kitten?"

"Uh-huh." Elsa nodded. "And then I found him under my bed. He likes it there. I think he feels safe."

"You've been hiding him in your

room?" Sara sounded shocked.

"Only since yesterday after breakfast." Elsa smiled at her sister. "He slept on my bed last night. Oh, shh, I think he's coming out."

They watched, holding their breath, as the black kitten crept forward. He paused at the very edge of the bed, eyeing Sara suspiciously.

"Don't be scared," Elsa whispered. "Come on…. Come on, Pepper…."

"You named him!" Sara shook her head. "Oh, Elsa. Dad is *not* going to let you keep him…."

"He might," Elsa said stubbornly as Pepper rubbed his head cautiously against her jeans. "You don't know."

"He is very cute," Sara admitted. "Can I pet him?"

"I don't know…." Elsa looked at Pepper doubtfully. "I had to tempt him out with food, but he's a lot less shy than he was. Maybe if we sit on the floor and keep still, he'll be brave enough to come closer."

Sara nodded and the two girls sat down, leaning against Elsa's bed. Pepper watched them for a moment, and then he clambered up onto Elsa's jeans and looked at Sara thoughtfully.

"Maybe we smell kind of the same to a kitten," Elsa whispered.

Sara rolled her eyes, but she was smiling, and when Pepper put one cautious paw onto her leg, she beamed. The tiny kitten sighed and then collapsed across their outstretched legs like a saggy, furry toy.

"You're going to have to tell Dad," Sara said, tickling the sleepy kitten under the chin.

"Can we wait a little while?" Elsa pleaded. "What if he says we can't keep him? I've had a kitten less than two days. I can't give him up yet." She leaned across to rub one finger over Pepper's velvet head. "Wouldn't you like to keep him?" she added coaxingly.

"Well … yeah…. He's beautiful," Sara admitted. "I've been asking Dad about getting a dog again, but I don't think he's going to say yes. He doesn't want to leave a dog alone at home while we're at school and he's at work. A kitten wouldn't mind that so much, would he?"

"No. Exactly!" Elsa said eagerly. "He'd be a perfect pet. So, will you help me persuade Dad then? Pepper would be the family's cat, not just mine."

Sara glanced over at the bedroom door, and Elsa could see her thinking it through—there were tiny frowns and then flickers of a smile. At last she gave a slow nod. "Okay. But I think we should tell him right away. The sooner the better. I don't think he's going to be happy that you kept Pepper a secret."

Elsa sighed. She'd been hoping to wait a little longer—until they were really settled in the house, and Dad wasn't so stressed about the move. But she knew Sara was right.

"Let's go downstairs," she said slowly. "Dad said he was going to do stuff online—changing addresses and that sort of thing. He said it was going to be really boring. He might like a break."

"You take him." Sara gently scooped Pepper off her lap. "He was yours first. But I'll definitely tell Dad I think we should keep him."

The two sisters walked slowly downstairs, with Elsa cradling Pepper against her cardigan. She just hoped Dad was in a good mood.

"You can't be looking for a snack already," Dad muttered as they came into the kitchen. He was glaring at his laptop, and Elsa almost backed out of the room, thinking it might be better to come down again later.

"We don't want a snack," Sara said, putting a hand on Elsa's back and pushing her forward a little. "Elsa found out what was making those weird noises."

Dad looked up. "Oh, no—not a rat!" Then he saw Pepper, blinking at him sleepily from Elsa's arms. "A kitten?"

"He must have been in the attic," Elsa explained.

"You didn't go up there, did you?" Dad asked worriedly. "That floor is wobbly, Elsa. It's dangerous."

"No, honestly. Pepper came downstairs. I found him under my bed."

"Pepper?" Dad frowned. "I'm guessing you haven't just found him, then, if he has a name."

Elsa looked at the floor and muttered, "It was yesterday morning. You were busy…. I didn't want to bother you…."

"Oh, Elsa…." Dad sighed. "He must be starving."

"I fed him pieces of sandwich, and cheese. He loves cheese—remember Grandma said how Patches really liked cheese? That's where I got the idea."

"She also said that if Patches had too much, she threw up all over the couch," Dad pointed out grimly. "At least you've been feeding him, I suppose. But where did this kitten come from? That's what I want to know. He couldn't have been in the attic by himself." His eyes widened. "Are there more of them up there? His mom, maybe?"

"I haven't heard them," Elsa said, shaking her head. She hadn't thought of going to look. "I think he was on his own."

Dad stood up. "I'd better go and check. You two stay here, please. I don't want you anywhere near those holes in the floor."

Elsa made a face at Sara as Dad

disappeared off upstairs. "Dad sounds really grumpy. We shouldn't have told him now. It was a really bad idea."

"He hasn't said no," Sara pointed out. "It might be okay." She reached over and tickled Pepper under his chin. "You need to put on your best cute face for when he comes back," she said. "Come on, kitten. Time to charm Dad."

Chapter Seven
An Unpopular Answer

Dad came back down saying that there were no more kittens upstairs, but he thought he could see where Pepper had been sleeping.

"It's a little smelly up there, too," he said, frowning. "I don't think he's house-trained."

Sara made a face, but Elsa shook her head. "I put down newspaper in my bedroom, Dad. He peed on it like he understood what it was for. And he pooped on the paper, too. I took it all out to the garbage can this morning and put some more down."

"I suppose that's something." Dad sighed. "But we need to find out who he belongs to, Elsa. We can't just adopt him."

"Can't we?" Elsa asked pleadingly. "He's really good, Dad. He's so friendly and sweet. Sara likes him, too." She elbowed her big sister, and Sara nodded.

"I think we should keep him. He's cute, Dad. You should try petting him."

"I thought you were desperate for a dog!"

Sara sighed. "I know. But you're right—it wouldn't be fair when we're out all day. Cats don't mind being left as much as dogs do. We could take care of a cat, no problem."

Dad shook his head. "We've only just moved, Sara. We've got enough to worry about without a cat, too."

Elsa swallowed hard. She'd really hoped Dad would like Pepper—that he'd at least think about keeping the kitten. How could he just say no right away?

Dad sighed. "I'll get in touch with Mrs. Bell, the lady who used to live here, and see if she knows anything. Someone must be looking for him. He could have owners who really want him back."

Elsa tickled
Pepper under
his chin and
didn't say anything. If
they'd let such a tiny
kitten wander off and
get stuck in an attic all on
his own, Pepper's owners
shouldn't be allowed
to have him back.

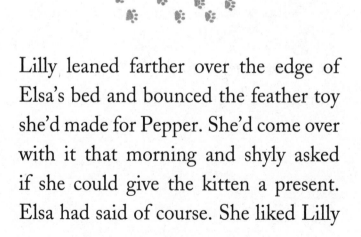

Lilly leaned farther over the edge of
Elsa's bed and bounced the feather toy
she'd made for Pepper. She'd come over
with it that morning and shyly asked
if she could give the kitten a present.
Elsa had said of course. She liked Lilly

a lot, and she was so glad she'd put that letter through her door.

Lilly had promised that she and her mom and Taylor, her little brother, would come and get Elsa and Dad on the first day of school, and that she'd make sure everybody knew who Elsa was. She said Elsa could sit with her and a couple of her friends at lunch, too. Elsa was feeling a lot less worried about the new school already.

"What was Mrs. Bell like?" Elsa asked. "My dad called the place where she's living yesterday, but she was sleeping. They're going to get her to call him back so he can ask about Pepper." She sighed. "At least it means we get to keep him for another day."

"She was nice," Lilly said slowly,

looking at Elsa. "I mean, she wasn't around that much. Mom said she was fragile and not very well. But if we saw her, she always said hello and smiled, and she remembered my name and Taylor's."

"So … she didn't seem like the kind of person who'd leave a kitten in an empty house?"

"No! Definitely not." Lilly looked horrified. "Is that what you think happened?"

"I don't know. I just don't know how Pepper got in, if he came from somewhere else—he's such a little kitten. I'm amazed he even got down the attic stairs. How could he have gotten into the house on his own?"

Lilly nodded. "I guess you're right. Though Mrs. Bell did have a cat, actually. We hardly ever saw her—she was *really* shy. But she was out in front of the house once, and Mrs. Bell told us that her name was Jemima and she was a stray cat who'd showed up in her yard. Maybe Pepper was Jemima's kitten!"

"It makes sense, doesn't it?" Elsa

looked puzzled. "But I don't see how somebody so nice could leave a kitten behind. If Dad calls her and she says she wants him back, I'm not sure we should let her have him."

"What are you going to do?" Lilly asked, wriggling around to stare at Elsa worriedly.

Elsa's shoulders slumped. "I don't know. If Dad says Pepper belongs to her, I guess we *have* to give him back."

Dad frowned at Elsa. "Look, I know you don't want to come—"

"It isn't that! I don't think we should be going at all," Elsa growled back. "She abandoned him!"

"We don't know that, Elsa. Mrs. Bell didn't sound very well on the phone, and she was really upset when I told her about Pepper. She asked if we could come and visit her, and I said we would. So we're going."

"But why did she leave him behind?" Elsa asked angrily. "It's so cruel! He would have starved if he hadn't come down the attic stairs and found us."

"I'm sure there's some reason," Dad said. "I know it seems odd. But I think we have to let her explain. She sounded so upset, Elsa. I honestly don't think she abandoned him on purpose. Anyway, if we go to see her, she'll be able to tell us, won't she?"

"Come on, Elsa." Sara gave her a

hug and whispered in her ear, "Stop arguing! We need to keep working on Dad to let us keep Pepper—you're not helping!"

Elsa shrugged on her coat. She was glad Sara was still hopeful, but she didn't think it was going to work. Dad seemed so determined to find Pepper's real home. She pulled her scarf out of the basket by the door, and Pepper leaped for the dangling fringe. Elsa couldn't help smiling, even though Pepper being cute just made her feel worse about losing him. "No, you can't have that, silly. I need it. Oh, Sara, look!"

Pepper was climbing up the scarf now, paw over paw, looking determined.

Dad shook his head. "I think he wants to come with you. Not this time, kitten. You need to stay here." He picked up the end of the scarf and Pepper, and tried to unhook the kitten's claws from the woolly fabric while Pepper squeaked angrily at him. "No, don't grab on again.... There! Okay, kitten, back in your box."

Dad carried Pepper to the kitchen and put him in the little cardboard box Sara had found. It was padded with an old towel, and it made a good temporary kitten basket. Then he hurried back along the hallway. "Okay, you two, quick. Out the door before he catches up with us." He shooed Sara and Elsa out and shut the door.

Pepper was still caught up in the folds of towel, stumbling his way out of the box and meowing anxiously. Where were they going? Why weren't they taking him, too? Elsa had left him alone in her room sometimes, but this felt different. All three of them were gone, and now the house felt cold and silent.

Beyond that big door, it smelled strange and a little scary. He didn't want to go out there, but he wanted to be left behind even less. They had all gone and abandoned him, just like his mother and the other kittens had. He stood by the front door and meowed anxiously, calling for Elsa to come and find him. He even scratched at the door with his claws, hoping it would open so he could run after her. He banged and scratched until his paws hurt, howling over and over. Why had they left? Where were they? Where was his mother?

At last he sank down onto the doormat, huddling in a limp little ball,

his sore
p a w s
tucked
u n d e r
his chest.
He was
so tired and so
cold. There was no one to cuddle up against. Pepper tucked his nose into the soft black fur of his chest, his breath shaky.

He was too small to understand that sometimes, people came back.

Chapter Eight
Mrs. Bell's Story

Elsa followed Dad and Sara and the nursing home assistant through the living room. She hadn't realized that Mrs. Bell had moved into a nursing home, but then Lilly had said she was very fragile.

The assistant crouched down beside an elderly lady in an armchair and gently patted her arm. "Mrs. Bell? I've brought

Mr. Parsons and his daughters to see you."

"Oh!" Mrs. Bell blinked as if she'd been half asleep and peered up at Dad and the girls. "Oh, thank you for coming. Bring some chairs over and sit down."

Dad pulled some chairs over and they sat down, looking rather uncomfortably at the elderly lady. No one knew quite what to say. Elsa was a little shocked that Mrs. Bell seemed so shaky and sick. How had she managed, living in their house—it really was starting to feel like their house now—with all the stairs? Maybe that was why she had left Pepper behind. She just hadn't been well enough to take care of him. But still….

"I was so shocked when you called me," Mrs. Bell began in a wavering voice. She looked at the three of them. "I'm so sorry. You really found a kitten in the house?"

"Yes." Dad nodded. "A little black kitten. Only a few weeks old, we think."

"Oh my goodness. I just don't understand," Mrs. Bell muttered.

"So … you didn't know he was there?" Dad asked uncertainly.

"No! Oh, no, of course not! If you hadn't moved in quickly, the poor little creature might have...." Mrs. Bell looked up at Dad in horror. "Did you think I'd abandoned him?"

Dad gave an uncomfortable shrug. "Well, we did wonder.... We weren't quite sure how it could have happened."

"What did happen?" Elsa asked. "Please. Where did Pepper come from?"

"Yes, I'd better explain. I don't really understand either, but—well, my beautiful cat, Jemima—" Mrs. Bell sniffed. "I'm sorry. It's still hard to talk about her. She was a stray. I found her in the backyard about a year ago. So thin and hungry, poor little thing. She was much too shy to come in, but obviously no one was feeding her, so

I bought some cat food and put it out for her in a little dish on the patio.

"It was wonderful seeing her get sleeker and happier, and eventually she got used to me. She moved into the house very slowly, you see. I think it was the cold that won her over—it snowed last year, and that was the first night she spent inside. She was never a lap cat, but she'd purr, and she had a little basket in the kitchen…."

"What color was she?" Elsa asked curiously, wondering if Jemima was a black cat like Pepper.

"Oh, a beautiful tabby, but brown, not gray. She was so pretty, such long whiskers…." Mrs. Bell's face twisted, and Elsa realized with horror that she was trying not to cry. What had happened to Jemima?

Mrs. Bell sniffed and went on. "I should have taken her to the vet to have her spayed and get her vaccinations done, but she was so shy that I didn't want to catch her and put her in a basket. She'd have been so scared. So I never got around to it. And then of course I realized she was a lot, lot fatter, and she was going to have kittens." Mrs. Bell sighed. "And by that time, I couldn't get up the stairs very well. Those steep stairs to the attic were just too much for me. I only went upstairs to bed, and sometimes if I wasn't feeling well, I slept on the couch. Then my daughter, Beth, came to see me, and she realized how difficult everything was getting, so she persuaded me to move here. I was ready to—all the meals cooked and people to talk to. It's wonderful…. Except…."

Dad nodded and then said gently, "Except you couldn't bring Jemima."

"Yes. Beth and I looked so hard for somewhere I could go that would let me have a cat, but there wasn't anywhere."

Mrs. Bell rubbed her eyes. "I arranged for the people from the animal rescue to come and get her," she explained. "She'd had her kittens—I could hear them squeaking— but I never saw

114

them because I couldn't get up the stairs. I just put a lot of food down for her—nice treats like pieces of chicken, so she had the strength to feed her babies.

"Beth went up and peered around the door and she said they were beautiful, all curled up with Jemima in a box of old clothes. She took a photo for me. And of course I saw them when the girls from the rescue took them away. Poor Jemima.... She was terrified."

Elsa sneaked her hand into Dad's. She'd been so angry about Pepper being left all alone—she hadn't imagined there would be such a sad story behind it. "But they didn't take Pepper?"

Mrs. Bell shook her head, wiping her eyes with her hand again. "Beth and I must have miscounted, that's all I can think of. We told the rescue people there were four kittens, and they found four kittens. All tabby. But maybe the little black kitten was hiding. They just didn't know to look for him. I'm so sorry. Thank goodness you found him."

"Yes." Elsa nodded earnestly. Then she added, "We weren't sure if you were going to want him back."

"I wish I could," Mrs. Bell said. "It broke my heart giving up Jemima, and I would have loved to keep the kittens, too. Though I would have made sure to get them all neutered or spayed, of course." She looked at Elsa and Sara and Dad hopefully. "Are you going to be able to keep him? If not, I can give you the phone number of the rescue where they took Jemima and his brothers and sisters."

Elsa turned to look at Dad, her eyes wide with hope, but he was nodding. "That would be really helpful. The girls really want to keep him, but I'm not sure we can manage a cat when we're still getting settled in the house."

Elsa blinked back tears, and she saw Sara's face fall. How could Dad still say that, even after hearing Jemima's sad story?

Both the girls were silent in the car on the way back. Sara didn't sit in the front with Dad, like she often did. Instead, she got in the back with Elsa and reached for her hand. They held on to each other all the way home.

"Look, I'm sorry," Dad said gently as he turned off the engine in front of the house. "I know you two want to keep Pepper. Maybe once we're more settled, we can look at getting a pet. Guinea pigs, like you wanted, Elsa, or we could think about a cat."

Elsa nodded, and sniffed, and she stumbled up the path after Dad and Sara, trying not to burst into tears. There didn't seem to be any point crying and arguing when Dad had made up his mind like this.

Then Dad pushed the door, and it bumped against a little ball of dark fur. Dad peered around and caught his breath worriedly. "Pepper!"

The kitten blinked up at them, limp and bedraggled, and then his eyes seemed to glow bright green. He sprang to his feet, meowing frantically.

"It hasn't been that long since Elsa fed you," Dad said, shaking his head. "Are you hungry already?"

"Oh, Dad...." Elsa scooped Pepper up, half laughing, half crying as he nuzzled desperately at her, nosing at her cheeks and chin. "I don't think he's hungry. Look at his paws. His claws are split. And there's a little bit of blood on this one."

"Look at the *door*...," Sara put in.

"We left him behind," Elsa said shakily. "Like Jemima and the other kittens did."

"You mean, he thought we were gone forever?" Dad reached out to pet Pepper very gently with one finger. *He looks shaken*, Elsa thought.

"He's been abandoned before," Sara said quietly.

Dad sighed and rubbed his hand across his face. "I suppose so. All right."

Elsa blinked at him. "All right what?"

"We'll keep him."

"What?" Elsa could feel her mouth gaping open, like a fish. "You mean it?" she whispered at last. When Dad nodded, she pressed her cheek against Pepper's fur, feeling a faint purr start up. She was holding on to him as tightly as she dared, and it didn't feel like enough.

Elsa reached over and lifted Pepper out of the Christmas tree—again. This time he came with a long strand of ribbon wrapped all around his paws.

"It's not a cat toy," she told him sternly, but Dad laughed.

"It's the best cat toy, Elsa. Jungle gym, jingly bells, nice squishy presents to land on if you fall out.... Speaking of which.... Here—open this one. It's for you and Sara. Sara, put your new phone down for a sec. Look at what Elsa's opening."

He handed Elsa a thin, flat package wrapped up in red paper, and Elsa started to tear it open curiously. She'd already opened her big present—the bike she'd asked for—plus a ton of cool stuff for Pepper, including a squishy igloo cat basket, which he'd completely ignored so far. She had no idea what this present could be, unless maybe it was a book about taking care of cats.

Sara helped her pull off the last of the paper, and the two girls stared down at a picture frame with a photo of a beautiful chestnut-brown tabby cat. She was beautiful, but very thin, and she had big, golden eyes. She was gazing at them out of the picture, and she looked worried.

"Oh! Is it Jemima?" Elsa asked,

remembering how Mrs. Bell had described her. "Is it for Pepper so he knows what his mom looks like?"

Dad was grinning at them. "There's an envelope!" he said, rubbing his hands excitedly. "You have to open the envelope, too."

"Oh...." Elsa picked it out of the wrapping paper and tore it open. Inside was a sheet of paper labeled *Adoption Certificate*. "'David, Sara, and Elsa Parsons, congratulations on adopting Jemima....'" she read. "Jemima? Dad! You went and got her from the rescue!"

"I really wanted to have her here on Christmas Day, but she's still feeding the other kittens," Dad explained.

"Anna, the lady who organized it all, said she's pretty sure the kittens will have new homes soon. Apparently they're very unusual, being born late in the year, so there aren't many kittens around wanting homes right now."

"And then Jemima can come back here." Elsa hugged him, but then she looked worried. "What about Mrs. Bell? Won't Jemima think it's weird if she's not around?"

"Possibly," Dad agreed. "But Anna seemed to think that she'd get used to it. She's very timid with the rescue staff, apparently, so Anna leaped at the chance for Jemima to go back to her old home, even if it's with different people. She thinks Jemima is more likely to settle in here than anywhere else. Though you have to realize that she'll probably never be as friendly as Pepper."

"I don't mind," said Elsa. "I hated it when Mrs. Bell said how scared she was, being brought to the rescue. And we could take photos and send them to Mrs. Bell, couldn't we?" she suggested.

"That's a very good idea." Dad looked happy with himself. "Good surprise?" he asked hopefully.

"The best!" Elsa reached down to grab Pepper, who was just about to leap into the lower branches of the Christmas tree again. "Pepper's going to think so, too. And if we have Jemima, then he won't be lonely when me and Sara are at school."

Pepper wriggled grumpily in her arms. Why wouldn't they let him climb that tree? It smelled good, and it was full of things that sparkled and jingled and rustled when he patted them with his paws. But every time he got anywhere near it, someone always whisked him away.

"Here, you can play with the ribbon you've already stolen," Elsa told him, dangling it over his nose, and Pepper lunged at it, hugging the ribbon close and growling at it fiercely. He was *not* going to give it back.

He lay there on Elsa's lap, wrapped up in ribbon and patting the glittery ends every so often. He was getting sleepy now. Trying to climb the tree so many times had worn him out. He yawned, showing all his tiny, needle-sharp teeth, and then purred as Elsa rubbed under his chin.

"You're staying with us, and now your mom's coming back, too," Elsa whispered. "We'll have two cats. Oh, I can't wait to tell Lilly."

Pepper purred sleepily and rolled over, snuggling up against Elsa's hand and nuzzling her. He stretched his paws over her fingers determinedly.

He wasn't letting her go.